Testing the Waters

Nicola Nichols

FIRST IMPRESSIONS

The view from the airplane amazed Shelly and in a wonderful way. The island she saw below them was exactly like the picture — the delicious tropical paradise the brochure had promised.

As the plane descended, she sighed at emerald green water surrounding the island. They flew over the small town where cruise ships came, but their destination was the other side of the island. A private area where there were no buildings except for the resort. Even that was hard to see, as it blended in with the palms beautifully.

"As advertised," she said breathlessly and with a certain amount of relief. In the next seat, Diane, her girlfriend, flashed her a smile. She'd been worried that the trip might be a rip-off too. They'd sweated blood to save for what was a wild extravagance.

A shuttle bus, driven by a smiling local man brought them from the airport. As they checked into their room, their excitement grew. They'd picked this resort carefully. It had been advertised as a place where young people met and partied. It was adults only, yet it deliberated left out some of the amenities that attracted older travelers. There were no fancy restaurants or relaxing bars with bands playing soft jazz.

No, this was a place that warned guests that there would be noisy parties and fun without hassles.

And so far, that seemed to be exactly what it was. Loud rock boomed from the poolside where they could see dozens of young and fit people crowding around. Many of the girls were topless, wearing only thongs, and there were fit-looking guys in speedos.

It filled them with the hope they'd have the vacation they wanted and had saved for.

In their room they quickly shed their travel clothes, dragging out new thongs and sandals from their suitcases. "Did you see all those buff guys in skimpy swimsuits?" Shelly said happily. "I just love the way they advertise their equipment."

"Did I see? Are you kidding? I was staring at the meat out by the pool when the bellman brought us to the room. And I think I fell in love at least three times walking through the lobby," Diane said.

"That's lust, not love," Shelly teased. She held up a finger. "Please remember that we are here on the catch and release program."

"A fishing metaphor? Please."

"Why not?" She pointed to her thong. "We brought bait and we are going to see what we can reel in. I'm not looking to take any of these guys home… although I might take back an email address or two if the catch measures up. But while I am here, I intend to focus on variety."

"Well, there seems to be plenty of variety here." Diane grinned nervously. "It's exciting and all, but now that we are here, and given our plan, I admit to experiencing a little tingle of guilt."

"Guilt?"

"Yeah. Telling our boyfriends that we were taking a cruise that was to study the culture…"

"I intend to study the local culture intimately," Shelly said.

"Well, given our goal, I wonder if they aren't going to be messing around while we are gone."

Shelly sighed. "So what?"

"What?"

"The whole reason we chose this, besides just to have a good time and get laid, is to get our heads straight. Both of those guys are pestering us to make a commitment and it's the big one — marriage."

"Bob said they want to make it a double wedding."

"They make agreeing sound like a no brainer. They like us, we like them and off we go. But before I take a step that big, I want some perspective."

"On what?"

"On me, mostly. I haven't even dated anyone but Charlie in a couple of years. And I didn't have that much experience with men, with sex, before I met him. Charlie is fun, but I'm scared to death that several years down the road I might find out that he's not the right guy."

"But you like him."

"Yet, my fantasies tell me I want more. I've never gone crazy and maybe I need to do that to make sure I'll be happy with Charlie forevermore."

"I suppose," Diane said.

"That's why we are here, in this tropical paradise. We came to a lovely, seductive place where they are out sight. Now we need to put them of our thoughts and do what we want for a time."

"Easier said than done."

"Diane, you can look at guys and dream about Bob if you want, but I intend to get fucked by more than one guy while I'm here. I want to find try out enough cocks to know for myself what I need. That way, when we get back, if I still want to marry Charlie, it will mean he's the guy I want and not just the first one to propose to me." Then she grinned. "If I have too much fun, then I'll keep my eyes open at home and start saving for another vacation."

Diane sighed. "You're right. I admit that part of my reluctance to marry Bob is that I find myself wondering, daydreaming about fucking other guys. I don't know if that's normal, but it's true."

"Bob seems hot."

"He seems so to me too, but my experience is limited."

Shelly giggled. "That means we need to do some extensive research into hot guys. I'm glad there seems to be a lot to choose from." She held up her thong. "I am going to bait the hook. I intend to advertise my assets and see what bites."

"What if several come on to you?"

"Then maybe I can fulfill another fantasy — having sex with more than one guy at a time."

"Really? You want to try that?"

"And you don't?"

"Well, I'm not sure." She grinned. "I've had fantasies of doing it."

"And it gets you hot."

Diane fidgeted. "Sure."

"Now you have a chance to find out. See, Diane, I need to know what I want from life, from sex, and how else do you find out except by trying out your options? We need to test the waters."

"Test what waters?"

"The wild waters. We need to see if the heat is what we really want. We need to find out if Bob and Charlie are the right choices, but we also need to learn if having just one man in our lives is what we really want."

Diane shivered, thinking about it. "Yeah."

"So here we are. And getting back to your rotten fishing metaphor and the idea of bait... a lot of the other girls were topless." Diane asked. "Are you intending to jump into the deep end?"

Shelley laughed. "Well, I certainly don't intend to let the other girls get the hot guys because I was modest." She laughed and tugged at her thong. "If things go according to plan, even though this doesn't hide much, I won't even have it on for long."

"You are ready to fuck the first hot guy who comes along and makes a pass?"

Shelly shrugged. "Damn right. We aren't going to be here long enough to waste time."

"So we go to the pool?"

"I'd kind of like to check out the beach," Shelly said.

Diane gave her an uncertain nod and, wearing thongs and sandals and carrying a towel, they headed for the beach.

When they got to the beach, a tall black woman wearing a sarong around her waist brought them a fancy and sweet drink with an umbrella in it. "A free rum punch for the new guests," she told them. "You girls have a great time." Her eyes twinkled. "Careful you don't burn those pale white titties."

They barely made it to a folding chair on the beach before two good looking guys came over to hover around. *I like this already*, Shelly thought as the guys chatted with them. She shaded her eyes from the sun and tried to get a clear glimpse of their crotches.

"You girls want to go to a party?" one named John asked.

"What kind of party?" Shelly asked. The idea appealed to her, but John didn't seem all that steady on his feet. She wondered if he might have already collected a few too many umbrellas from drinks.

"There is a meet and greet this evening at the pool at six." His eyes groped her breasts. "The resort puts it on to give everyone a chance to scope out the other guests. There are free booze and finger food."

"Sounds great," Diane said unenthusiastically.

"Great," he said. Then the two men wandered off.

Shelly watched them go with astonishment. "That's it?"

"When he first mentioned a party, I thought he was going to try to get us up to his room," Diane said.

"Me too. I was hoping he meant in his room. They had us right where we wanted us," Shelly said.

"They are nerds, of course."

Shelly snorted. "They still have dicks, and you'd think that would give them a few better ideas."

They watched people milling about, feeling a little less enthusiasm. After a while, they ate an early dinner in the beach-front restaurant and then, for lack of a better alternative, went to the party.

The party was held around the pool. A DJ played music, but no one danced. Most of the people huddled in groups, talking.

"It's hopeless," Shelly said after trying to mingle for a time.

"What?"

"These guys. I should have known that advertising aimed at corporate types would result in guys like these."

"There are some are nice looking guys here," Diane pointed out.

"I know. And here I am, standing in front of them wearing nothing but a thong and so far the guys coming up to me have asked what company I work for and what kind of software I write."

Diane grinned. "You knew it would mostly be the tech industry crowd. When it comes to people our age, they're the ones who can afford to go places like this."

"Yeah, but I didn't know they would bring the industry along on vacation," Shelly said. "I thought they'd be out for pussy and they are busy networking."

"Play the odds," Diane said.

"What odds. When these morons have met their business card quota most of them will just snort some coke and pass out early. What the fuck good is that? I didn't spend all that money and travel this distance to talk shop with guys who don't even stare at my tits."

"It's a disappointment, but it's early."

"Well, I have to say Charlie is looking pretty fucking good at the moment. He'd have fucked me by now." Then she turned and walked toward the beach. Diane ran after her and caught up with her just outside the fringe of the party.

"Where are you going?"

"For a walk on the beach. I need to get away from this for a bit and maybe go for a swim."

"But the party…"

"You go back to that cute guy I saw you making out with earlier. I'll be okay."

"He passed out drunk," Diane said. She took a look at the crowd that milled around the pool. "The rest are decent eye candy with no substance. I might as well join you."

"For what we are paying, we should at least be able to walk around nearly naked at night on the warm sand."

BEACH BUMS

More disappointed than anything else, Shelly took off her sandals and then led Diane away from the lights around the pool. She wanted to hear the roar of the ocean and let the Caribbean lap her feet. The sand was cooler and harder by the water's edge.

When they stopped and turned to look back at the resort, they saw two men watching the party from the shadows.

"Enjoying the show?" Shelly asked.

"Trying to figure it out," one said. He turned to face her, and his eyes took in her naked breasts.

Finally. The man was a bit older than the crown by the pool. And big. He was at least six-five and had black skin that reflected the light. The dim light helped make him look sexy, but his muscular body, arms that seemed to bulge even though he stood relaxed, didn't need fancy lighting. "They do this every week," he said making it sound as old and tired as it Shelly had found it.

"It's a meet and greet," Diane said.

The man shifted his gaze to slowly run it over both of their bodies.

"I can think of lots better ways to greet half-naked women than with a limp-dick party like that sucker," the other man said.

Shelly smiled at him. "Can you?"

This one was stockier and shorter with thick yellow hair that came nearly to his shoulders. Both men wore shorts and nothing else. Shelly thought they were both hot.

The man snorted. "Shit yes. I saw you two trying to get some kind of attention and the dolts didn't have a clue that you weren't there to chit chat."

"Then tell me, what kind of ways to greet women come into your non-doltish mind?" she said, teasing.

Diane nudged her.

The yellow-haired man flashed an inviting smile. "Lots of things. A simple show of appreciation, like saying 'nice tits' maybe, or suggesting a walk on the beach to fuck under the stars and the soft light of the quarter moon."

"Yuck; sand in the butt crack," Diane laughed.

The yellow-haired man smiled and held out his hand. "My name is Jock," he said, "and my friend is Paul. We live on the beach and I can assure you, without fear of contradiction, that, with practice, you can learn to have wonderful sex on the beach without getting sand in your butt crack. At least not enough to spoil the fun."

Diane looked up at him. "You live on the beach?"

Jock nodded. "For a while now. It works out well. The landlord is a great bloke and it makes for a short commute to the office," he laughed.

"What the hell do you do?" Shelly asked.

"We are entrepreneurs. We collect the curious and interesting things, natural and manmade that the tide kindly deposits on the sand and them into trinkets, jewelry and stupid shit that tourists buy at the market on the other side of the island."

"That sounds like a weird way to make a living," Diane said.

He smiled. "Weird? Not really. Uncertain and flakey it probably is. In fact, I'm sure it is, but it lets us live on the beach."

"Don't believe them," Shelly said. "They are probably programmers on vacation."

Jock laughed. "Bad guess. We speak the truth. We really are professional beach bums, although, for tax evasion purposes, we prefer to be called beachcombing agents."

"And you live on the beach?" Shelly asked, making it something of a challenge.

"On the beach," Paul said. "In the antithesis of lavish elegance. Want to see how the other one percent lives?"

They did want to see. "Why not?" she said, and even Diane was interested enough to stop fretting.

As they headed down the beach, walking at the edge where the water tasted their toes, just as she'd wanted, Shelly found their new companions even more attractive than she'd first thought.

She moved close to Paul as the men led them down the dark beach. The stars were bright, but the moon was small and thin — a mere wisp of a crescent trapped between light clouds.

As night came on, the air cooled a bit and she grew more aware of the heat radiating from Paul's body. Given that she had started this trip on the prowl, the proximity of a man was getting her hot.

She had never had sex with a black man but she sure was wondering what it would be like to do it with this one. Part of her arousal was simply the novelty of the situation, the erotic tropical setting and all that, not to mention being almost naked. But beyond that, Paul exuded a sexiness that was really getting her wound up.

As they walked in the dark, his arm moved around her waist and his hand rested on her hip. She shivered as his long fingers touched her bare ass. The thong was no protection. Her cunt began to tingle.

"Home at last," Paul said as they reached a clearing where two small tents were pitched. It was a makeshift camp at best, but Shelly wasn't worrying much about that.

Suddenly she realized that Jock and Diane had lagged behind. She heard their muffled voices and smiled. Despite her claim that she felt guilty about the purpose of their trip, Diane was giggling and enjoying whatever he was saying. When her friend let out a surprised gasp of pleasure, it became more a question of what he was doing to her.

Paul stopped at an outcrop of rock and turned to face Shelly. Waves tickled her feet as he put a hand under her chin and lifted her face, looking into her eyes. She looked up at him and his hands caressed her ass as he bent his face down and kissed her. His warm lips made her moan and then his tongue filled her mouth. The hands on her ass pressed her body pressed against his and she felt the hard bulge of his cock.

When he broke the kiss, he leaned her back gently a smooth curve of rock that was still warm from the sun. His mouth was suddenly hot on her nipple, his thick tongue and lips massaged it as his fingers undid the ties of her thong.

She sighed as it dropped to the ground and the night air caressed her cunt.

He switched his warm mouth to her other nipple, and she arched her back, wanting him to suck it. As it spread tendrils of desire through her, she reached for his shorts and did them. When they dropped to his knees, her hand grasped his long and hard cock.

"Fuck," he moaned, then he dropped to his knees. He pressed his face into her pussy and his tongue set fire to her belly. His hands caressed her hips and then grabbed them. He lifted her ass, pushing her up further on the rock. As she rocked back, she opened her legs for him, wanting more of that tongue burning in her cunt. When he was eating her, she wrapped her legs around his head, crossing her ankles behind him.

She clung to him as his tongue and lips attacked her clitoris, his fingers working in her pussy. Soon, he brought her to a climax, continuing to devour her as she shuddered and moaned with pleasure.

When she began to unwind, reluctantly unwrapping her legs, she opened her eyes and saw sparkling stars in a dark sky, and Paul's lusty smile — the twinkle in his eyes echoing the night sky.

She looked down and saw his swollen cock in a massive hand. It loomed large in front of him as he moved up and brought it to her wet cunt. She wanted it throbbing inside her more than ever now; as his hands pulled her thighs toward him, she opened her legs again, this time wrapping them around his waist as he entered her.

His cock burned wonderfully as it penetrated her deeply. She hooked her legs behind him and pulled him tight and felt his lusty shaft filling her. He ground her ass against the rock as he fucked her.

The spray from an occasional wave slapping against their rock splattered her with salt as Paul gave her exactly what she had come to the island for — a serious fuck that wasn't Charlie.

He was strong, like the sea, and nearly as relentless. Then, when he came, his beautiful ebony prick erupting in her cunt, he roared with the waves. The surge of the incoming tide of cum roared up inside her.

"Fuck," she sighed.

Shelly and Paul gathered up their clothes and walked from the beach up to the tents. As they got to the camp, Diane and Jock ran by them, naked, wet and salty. "Skinny dipping is fantastic after a good fuck," Diane giggled as they sat on blankets outside the tents.

They were all naked now, and although it was warm, Paul built a small fire. They sat around in the flickering light. It was erotic. When Jock moved close to her, she felt a bittersweet tang. She expected to fuck Jock, but she also wanted Paul. Fuck, she wanted both of them.

This vacation was far too short, too precious to waste and both of these guys met her criteria for partners for the kind of sexual experience she wanted. As he put an arm around her, his hand on her breast, she reached to his lap and let her fingers touch his cock. The thought struck her that this soft prick had been inside Diane's cunt just a short time ago. As she wondered how long before he'd feel desire again, that tool began to respond, quickly growing thicker than Paul's. Thick, although probably a tad shorter.

"You girls are arousal magic," Jock said and he kissed her breasts. "I should've known. Sea nymphs like you can overwhelm a man's feeble senses any time."

She liked the thought; even more, she liked the feel of the fingers he had slipped between her legs.

As she bent her knee and moved her leg to give him more room to tease her wet pussy, still damp with Paul's cum, she slumped against his powerful chest. "Now that is magic," she sighed as his fingers danced in her cunt, making her tremble.

With her legs apart and his fingers inside her, Shelly let her own fingers trace the hard muscles of this man's chest. If Paul was the athlete of the pair, wiry and strong, then Jock was the muscle man. Which kind of man would make a better lover?

Testing the Waters

The proof was in the fucking, and she intended to find out.

But now Jock put her on her back on the blanket and kissed her. Then he ran his hands down, over her, making her tingle. Those strong hand grasped her thighs in a firm grip and he bent her legs far back toward her breasts. She held her calves and watched as he bent his face and put his tongue on her thighs, burning.

She moaned as that wild tongue traced an erotic trail directly into her cunt. He pressed his face tight against her as his tongue penetrated her. Then he moved his tongue up her cunt so slowly that she thought she might go crazy. When he reached her clitoris, he sucked the hard nun in his mouth and rubbed his tongue against it.

With her legs pinned back, all she could do was reach between them and grab his ears, pulling his face to her. His tongue began gently flicking her clitoris; each flick lifted her up like the rollers on the beach. He shoved his fingers inside her, fucking her with them and adding to her arousal.

She cried out, almost with surprise, as he brought her to climax. She had never come twice so soon before.

Then his body loomed over her. He held her legs and drove his thick cock into her with a knee-melting ferocity. She thought she actually felt his need to fuck her, to come in her. And she wanted it too.

His powerful thrusts drove her into the sand as he buried his prick in her. Once or twice her cervix protested. She focused on making her cunt muscles try to trap that wild prick, to caress it.

She was gasping for air when he finally came. The hard jerks of his hips slammed his body into hers and then he stopped, moaning as his spunk flooded her.

When he had come and his weight rested on her, Jock surprised her by stroking her cheek tenderly, then kissing her and calling her his sea nymph again.

She looked to the blanket beside them. Paul was kneeling behind Diane, taking her in long strokes. Her ass cheeks reflected the moonlight. With each thrust into her pussy, she made primal sounds that might have been delightful obscenities if they had been intelligible, but her face was muffled — pressed into the blanket. Her hand was between her legs as she ensured her own climax.

"Will you come back to our room?" Shelly asked Jock as they watched.

He shrugged. "It depends."

She kissed his chest. "On what? I want more of this," she said. "I am a greedy sea nymph."

"We need to collect stuff later today right after the tide changes," he said laughing. "We have to make some money too. But we might come in the evening."

"Mmm," she said as she watched Paul come in her girlfriend's cunt and the two of them collapse on their blanket.

"If you want more…" he laughed, putting her hand on his cock. She felt it stirring and sighed. "Talk to it," he said. "Tell it nice things."

She let herself slip down so that she could take it in her mouth and suck him hard. Happily, he responded and soon she had a rigid prick in her mouth.

"It turned you on to see your friend taken that way," he said when she looked up at him.

"Yes," she said.

He put her on her hands and knees. "Rear entry is sweet."

As he slipped his cock into her, she felt it press tight against her g spot and she sighed.

He knew what he was doing, that Jock. He fucked her powerfully and steadily. After coming twice, he was pacing himself.

Testing the Waters

She heard Paul and Diane talking and knew they were watching Jock fuck her, thrusting that spear between the petals of her pussy. That was hot. Her climax built, and she came, moaning, with her face pressed against the blanket and her ass pointing up toward the stars.

He held his prick inside her, but then he withdrew and pressed the thick head of his cock against her anus.

"Oh fuck," she moaned as she felt it stretching the tight ring open. It was a rush, knowing she was about to take that thick cock back there too. She had done anal before, but it was still a novelty.

Jock's shaft felt enormous and hard and hot; she wanted it and she pushed her hips back, felt him pushing forward and their bodies met with his cock deep in her ass. She gave a soft cry as he began moving in a lusty rhythm that moved his cock back and forth in her ass. The sensations that flesh of his aroused in her ass were amazing.

Her head spun with delight, with new experience. Suddenly, Jock slapped her ass. It startled her, and then he grunted, and she felt his spunk blasting up inside her rectum.

Much later, Paul and Jock began getting ready to comb the beach.

"You have the room number?" Diane asked.

Paul grinned. "Engraved in my heart."

"Tease. The door will be unlocked."

"That can be dangerous," Jock said.

"Only if randy men found out about it," Shelly said. "I hope some do."

As the men picked up burlap sacks and went off to what passed for work, the girls returned to the resort for desperately needed showers and sleep.

"So you think they will come?" Diane asked as they walked along the beach, feeling weak and weary and happy.

"With guys like that you never really know, do you?" Shelly said. It dawned on her that the unpredictability was part of their allure.

PARTY OF FOUR

After a long, hot shower, Shelly slept like a rock. She probably would've slept right through dinner, except for that hand — the hand that was running over her breasts and then down to her pussy.

"She's awake now," Paul said.

As her eyes flickered open, his smiling face moved down and his lips captured hers at the same moment his fingers worked their way into her pussy.

"Two randy guys, showing up to make things dangerous, as requested," Jock laughed.

Shelly glanced at Diane's bed and saw her lying face down and Jock, also naked, lying beside her, stroking her bare back. Diane just moaned softly as his hands traced the curves of her ass. His stiff prick rubbed against the back of her thigh.

After a bit, Jock rolled Diane over and turned her sideways on the bed, standing between her legs.

"We decided you sexy girls would enjoy a party for four," Paul said. He grabbed Shelly and led her over to the girl and pushed her down on her in a sixty-nine.

Jock grabbed her hair and put the tip of his cock to her lips. "Get it wet before I fuck her," he said.

She opened her mouth and he pressed the shaft into her mouth. As she sucked it, Jock smiled. "Paul's doing the same with your girlfriend, fucking her mouth. But now…" he pulled his cock out, then guided it to the pussy below Shelly's face. As she watched the throbbing flesh spread Diane's cunt open and disappear inside it, Paul moved his up to drive it into her own pussy.

The guys fucked them hard, rocking her on Diane's naked body. She could feel Diane's panting breath on her cunt as Paul took her.

When Jock came, he pulled his prick out and shot the last of his cum over Diane's pussy and Shelly's face. Paul tensed and came, sending his seed up her cunt and then leaning over to kiss her back.

Jock touched Shelly's cheek. "Eat her pussy clean," he said.

"And you do Shelly," Paul told Diane.

Shelly licked the cum from her mouth and put her face to Diane's pussy.

Another new thing in this grand adventure.

Shelly had sex with a girl before. But then, this vacation was all about new things, things she hadn't tried. And apparently, with these hot men, testing the waters meant tasting the pussy. She was willing to give it a try.

Diane had told her that she'd tried eating pussy once in college, and while she liked having a girl go down on her, she preferred it with men. But now, on this erotic vacation and with two men watching, and their cunts already full of cum, it was an irresistible experiment in the new.

As she ran her tongue through Diane's folds, it was easy to tell that the girl was definitely getting aroused by it all. She was too. Diane's tongue seemed to be everywhere, and when she added her fingers to the mix, it was incredible.

She tried to do her part, to get her fingers and tongue working together, but increasingly it was hard to focus. "Let her make you come, then you can finish her off," Jock whispered.

Testing the Waters

As it happened, getting Shelly off didn't take much. Paul's fingers toying with her asshole took her over the top and she writhed, squirming on her girlfriend as her orgasm rushed through her.

Then the men moved her, turning them both so that they could watch her on her knees between Diane's long legs, bending her face down to eat the girl's pussy. Paul stretched out alongside Diane, playing with her tits while he watched, and Jock fondled Shelly's ass.

Despite the distraction of Jock's hands, Diane's screams of pleasure told her she was doing a decent time eating pussy for the first time. And, by the time she lifted her damp face from Diane's cunt, she saw that the men were hard again. Paul rolled Diane on her side and lifted her legs. Shelly reached up and held his cock to guide it into her warm, wet snatch.

As she watched Diane's cunt take that prick, Jock held Shelly's upraised ass and worked his cock into her pussy, filling her wonderfully.

The two men fucked them on that small bed, taking their time now, enjoying the feel of thrusting in their pussies. "So warm and wet," Jock said, leaning over Shelly's back to whisper the words, warm and wet themselves, in her ear. "My cock loves it inside you."

The words made her tremble. They were crude, sincere, and exactly what she wanted to hear right then. "Then come inside me and later you can do it again," she told him. "Fuck me good."

And he did.

Nicola Nichols

MORNING IN PARADISE

When Shelly woke, the sun was high. Paul snored beside her; Jock was asleep, alone in Diane's bed.

Shelly smiled. Diane was a diehard runner — an addict. Running on the beach in the morning would be irresistible to her, even after a night like the last one. She'd already missed two mornings and would want to get back on schedule.

Her loss. As she sat up, her cell phone rang. It was John, the yuppie who had invited them to the party. She took the phone and went into the bathroom, sitting on the toilet to pee.

"I missed you at the party," he said.

"That's your fault. You were passed out when I arrived," she told him. "You missed everyone."

He laughed weakly. "I guess so. Partying, you know?"

"And now?"

"Well, a bunch of us rented a charter boat. Do you girls want to go sailing? We are thinking of taking a lunch and eating it on a deserted island. The crew takes care of the food and booze, and the details — like actually finding the island."

"How many are in a bunch?"

"If you two come along there would be eight of us. Two other girls."

She thought about it. "That might be fun," she said. Sailing was an activity she could enjoy and if there were six other people, plus a crew, there might be some interesting playmates. "Diane isn't here right now and I am just waking up. Can I call back?"

"We leave at one in the afternoon, but if you let me know any time before then that works."

Shelly sighed. Sailing was a nice fall back if Paul and Jock left to go do their work. Just then, Paul walked into the bathroom and watched her pee.

"Diane is off somewhere," she said.

"Running and laughing and splashing, she said," Paul said. "She told me she'd be back for breakfast."

"I need a shower," she said, standing.

"I need this," he said, slipping his arm around her.

"I stink."

"You smell like sex. You are just going to get stinkier."

"She sure is," Jock said. He was sporting a stiff prick and smiled when he saw Shelly looking at it. "I woke up dreaming of you two with your legs spread wide and inviting, only to find I was in bed alone. Fortunately, you are here, and one woman can accommodate two horny guys."

"In several ways," Paul agreed.

Shelly shivered. She'd woken up horny too and just looking at Jock's deliciously hard cock was getting her wet; this talk of them both fucking her was making her dizzy. "I've never…"

"Soon," Paul said, "you won't be able to say what you were about to say."

Weak with desire, Shelly let them lead her out of the bathroom and to the bed. Jock stretched out on his back, that stiff rod standing proudly erect. Shelly got on her knees and grabbed it, then began licking it tasting the heady mix of flavors of his cum and traces of her and Diane's pussies.

Behind her, Paul's face pressed into her hungry cunt and she gasped as he licked her. Then she took Jock's prick in her mouth and began sucking him while Paul's finger fucked her.

"Enough of the first course," Jock said. He grabbed her shoulders and pulled her up to straddle him, her pussy poised over his throbbing prick. With him balancing her, she squatted down, holding his shaft, bringing it to her swollen lips and then easing herself down on it.

Paul's strong fingers spread her ass cheeks apart, and as she filled her cunt with Jock's prick, he put his face to her anus and licked it, his hot, wet tongue sending incredible sensations shooting through her.

Jock laughed and pinched her nipples. "I think she likes it," he said.

She did. Her body was vibrating with the wildness of being fucked by one man while another licked her asshole. She ground her hips down on Jock, pushing her cunt against him. And then Paul moved, straddling her ass. She felt the hot touch of his cock on her anus. "I'm going to fuck this sweet ass," he said, his voice husky.

She cried out as he impaled her ass, his cock rubbing against Jock's in her pussy. She was trapped between the two men, with Paul setting the pace, thrusting down into her asshole. Jock bucked his hips in an erotic counterpoint that changed the interaction.

Shelly was taking two hard cocks at once for the first time in her life — and loving it.

"Oh God!" she cried out, feeling both cocks were moving in her. She knew that if she had ever imagined anything could feel so fucking good she would have done this long before.

As the men rocked her between them, the door opened. A sweaty Diane came walking in.

"Oh good," she said. "I didn't know the hotel had hard cocks available as room service." She flopped on the bed so that she could get a close look. While she watched the men fuck her friend, Diane squeezed one of Shelly's nipples.

"She is loving what you guys are doing," Diane said. "Fuck her hard."

Shelly moaned her agreement; she really did love having these two men fuck her while Diane watched. Somehow, having her best friend watch her fucked by two guys that she had also fucked made it more exciting.

Paul came first, his body thrashing on top of her, his seed flooding her asshole. When he moved away, Jock rolled her over, mounting her and using his cock like a pile driver in her pussy. By the time Paul came, his cum shooting down into her, Shelly collapsed, limp.

"I ordered breakfast from room service," Diane said. "We need to refuel."

"Are you interested in meeting other people while on thus vacation?" Paul asked as they finished eating breakfast. "As nice as this room is, I can't see staying inside all the time when there are some interesting local sights."

She wondered what sort of people he was thinking of. "I thought you weren't impressed with the people here. Are you saying we need to circulate — hang out with other guests at the hotel?"

"If that's what you want. But as charming as hanging with the nerds sounds, Jock and I really thought that you might like to meet some local people. The only ones you'll meet here are maids and bartenders who aren't supposed to socialize with the guests. No, we were thinking about heading down to an oil down this afternoon."

"An oil down?"

"It's a big party that is theoretically about food. Mostly though it is an excuse for people to get together. Not a meet and greet, you understand. In the early hours, it's a family thing. Later, however, it gets rowdy, even a bit rough. So not for the faint of heart."

Shelly licked her lips. "Sexy local people?"

He laughed. "That's for you to say. I'll say that I find a number of the local women damn sexy. The girls tell me that the guys are hot, and I have to admit that some of them have roguish good looks if you are into rastas, especially."

"So, you enjoy fucking the local girls as well as tourists?" Diane asked.

"Can't say that those qualities, local and tourist, have much to do with my interest. Nice legs, a compact ass, firm breasts, a tight pussy... now those are the things that make me enjoy fucking a woman."

"I need a shower," Diane said. She peeled off her shorts and top, then headed for the bathroom with a twitch of her ass. Jock sighed loudly as he stared after Diane's bare ass.

"It's a well-known fact that most domestic accidents take place in the bathroom," he said. "I better go make certain that she is all right. Besides, I want some of that sweet ass." And he hopped up and followed her in.

Shelly and Paul went to sit on the bed, leaning against the headboard and fondling each other. She was getting him quite hard again and feeling desire welling up her cunt to feel it inside again when the phone rang. She smiled at Paul and watched him raise his eyebrows. She took his stiff cock in her hand and crawled up over him, straddling his body as she picked up the phone.

It was John, sounding desperate. "Shelly, last chance to go sailing."

She looked at the stiffening cock in her hand. "That's sweet of you to check back but we can't make it, John." She grinned at Paul who put his hands behind his head and watched her with a smile. "Some other friends invited us to go for a ride."

"There are horses on the island?"

"At least two wild stallions," she said. She got up and straddled Paul's lap, then eased herself down. Paul held her as she put the tip of his cock between the lips of her pussy and began to sink down on it. She sighed audibly with the familiar sensation of being filled with a hard cock. "We only know of these two and they are good rides, but this evening our friends are taking us to see if we can find more."

"Don't fall off," John said.

"There will be oil, but falling off is not a worry," she said and hung up.

She was on her knees now, moving her hips, making that cock move inside her, rub it against the sweet spots in her cunt. It was delightful knowing she could ride his cock for a long time before he would come again. No, there was no way she'd fall off this mount.

As she fucked her black lover, sounds came from the bathroom over those of the shower. "Oh God, you fuck my ass so good, Jocko," she heard Diane moaning in the bathroom.

"Such a nice, tight ass," he moaned.

It didn't seem that Diane would prefer going sailing either. Sheila sighed happily, tightening the muscles of her cunt, squeezing Paul's cock.

Later she would think about what she'd learned from this adventure but right now she had a glorious cock inside her. She bent further forward, then gasped as Paul pushed a finger in her ass.

"Just testing the waters," he said, laughing as Shelly's body began to convulse with pleasure.

HOMEWARD BOUND

Shelly was groggy as she pushed the big Rasta off of her. Before he collapsed, he had fucked her ass while his friend came in her mouth. Maybe it was the ganja, but no one had last so long in her ass before.

And his hadn't been the first new cock of the evening, either. In the last few days it seemed like she'd fucked half the local men on the island.

It was dawn now, and she saw Diane walking around, naked, looking dazed.

"Can't find my clothes," she said.

Shelly shook her head. All the days since Paul and Jock had introduced them to the locals had blurred together. The oil down had quickly become an orgy and it was repeated several times. The girls had lost track of all the men who'd fucked them. They couldn't remember the last time they'd slept in the expensive beds in the resort.

They didn't care, either.

"I think we left our stuff under a palm tree," Shelly said, brushing sand off her ass. Then she remembered. "That one," she said, pointing and laughing. "It's the palm tree that is now underwater." The tide had come in and their clothes were gone.

Scrounging around in the aftermath of the party, they found tee-shirts that were way too big and could act as nightgowns. "They smell like shit, but they're good enough to go back to the room with," Shelly said.

"I've lost three nice skirts this week," Diane pouted.

"And enjoyed it every time."

Diane made a face, then laughed. "Yeah, there is that."

As they walked back, Diane said what was hanging between them, coloring the pleasure. "We leave this afternoon."

"I know. Fuck."

"On the bright side, we did what we came to do."

Shelly beamed. "If you mean getting fucked in every hole by a variety of guys and having our pussies eaten... yeah, we did."

"Money well spent. My body is sore. I think my pussy needs a rest anyway."

Shelly grinned. "So... if you were offered another night here for free and the airline would change the flight..."

"I'd do it in a heartbeat. I don't think I've tried that guy who did your ass this morning."

"He stayed hard for a long time."

"That's what I thought."

"So, we did it," Shelly said. Then she scowled. "And I still have no idea what I'll do about Charlie."

"Same for me. I care about Bob but, I sure liked screwing more than one guy." She grinned. "I had no idea how good it would be to get screwed by several at once."

"I'll say. We were the life of the party a few times."

"The life of a few parties." Diane screwed up her face. "Paul said either of us was welcome to stay with him. Tickets can be canceled."

Testing the Waters

Shelly shook her head. "That's not exactly a real alternative. I like some creature comforts. Besides, the hot sex is here, but everything else is at home."

"We've never really looked, though, have we?"

"Looked?"

"For hot sex at home. I mean, I've always dated guys thinking I was looking for a boyfriend. When we came here, I expected to find out if he is the right guy. But trying all these new things makes me wonder if I was asking the right question."

"Which is?"

"Do I want a boyfriend at all? The kind we thought we wanted. Here we were willing to meet guys purely for sex. At home, we probably ignored a dozen Pauls and Jocks. I'll bet we could find guys like that at home easily enough."

"That's a good point," Shelly said. "And we can string the guys along while we find out."

Diane sucked her finger. "As a way of testing the waters, checking out possibilities, maybe we could hint around about a foursome and see how they react? Who knows how wild they are willing to get?"

Shelly laughed. "The grass might be greener at home?"

"I think we need to investigate."

"So, we are back to testing the waters," Shelly said.

"Don't make it sound like you don't want to. You didn't seem to mind the strenuous effort here."

"I didn't mind getting well fucked."

Diane sighed. "And now, after talking about it, I am going to need a hot shower."

"That's easy enough."

"The problem is that I know I'm going to need to have you eat my pussy before we check out to go to the airport."

"I beg your pardon?"

"Oh, I'll eat you too… after you shower. You stink of half the men on the island right now."

"I do. This was a nice resort, wasn't it?"

"it was a really good choice," Diane agreed. "About perfect."

THE END

ABOUT THE AUTHOR

Nicola is always watching people, studying their interactions and excited by life and the many contradictory impulses we all contend with... wanting things we shouldn't, enjoying guilty pleasures, and fantasizing about the things we haven't dare to try.

If you enjoyed this story, please leave a review

And check out these sexy stories by Nicola Nichols

Anna Blows Town
Cocktail Party
Doing Her Husband's Crew
Lusty Hotwife Adventures
Taken on the "A" Train
Watching Me With Bikers